TIMEOUT!

HEADS UP, FOOTBALL FANS.

HEAD-TO-HEAD FOOTBALL is a very different kind of book; it can be read frontwards or backwards. Start from one end and you'll get the inside stuff on Detroit Lions' all-star running back, Barry Sanders. Or start from the other side to get the lowdown on the Dallas Cowboys' record-setting running back, Emmitt Smith.

Whichever way you begin, you'll want to read *both* superstar stories before tackling the amazing middle section of the book. See how Emmitt and Barry both overcame their small size to do big things on the football field. Read how, year in and year out, they battle each other for the NFL rushing title. Then check out the fantastic photos, stats, and comic strip that show just how these gridiron greats stack up against each other.

Okay, it's time for the coin toss. So pick Barry or Emmitt and get ready for all the Head-to-Head action!

BARRY SANDERS

By Craig Ellenport

A *Sports Illustrated For Kids* Book

Bantam Books

NEW YORK • TORONTO • LONDON • SYDNEY • AUCKLAND

CONTENTS

POETRY IN MOTION

The great athletes in team sports have the ability to take over a game. Sports people call it "being in the zone." Everything they do on the field works. The opposing team can't do anything to stop them. For a while, they become the perfect player.

Very few people get into the zone. The greatest athletes get there more often than anyone else. Michael Jordan does it, and so does Wayne Gretzky. On November 24, 1991, Barry Sanders, the star running back of the Detroit Lions, did it, too.

On that day, the Lions faced the Minnesota Vikings in Minneapolis, Minnesota. The Lions and Vikings play in the National Football Conference (NFC) Central division. The division has always been a tough one, with strong rivalries. The teams often play close, physical games.

This was a very big game for both teams. Going into the game, the Lions had a record of 7–4, their best that late into the season in 20 years. They trailed the first-place Chicago Bears by two games.

The Vikings had a record of 6–6 and needed a win to

have any chance of making the playoffs. They were known for their tough defense. Earlier in the season, the Lions had barely beaten the Vikings, 24–20. Barry had run 15 yards with only 36 seconds left for the winning score. Could Barry repeat his excellent performance in this game?

I n their first drive of the game, the Lions used Barry as a decoy, to try to fool Minnesota. He did not touch the ball until their fifth play. When Barry finally got a handoff, he ran left for eight yards. On his next carry, he got six more. The Lions were marching downfield.

On first down at the Vikings' 17-yard line, Barry took a handoff from quarterback Erik Kramer. He darted through a hole up the middle and ran 17 yards for a touchdown! The first quarter ended with Detroit in the lead, 7–0.

At halftime, the Lions were up 10–7. Barry had 60 yards on nine carries — and he wasn't even warmed up yet.

Detroit got the ball first in the second half. Barry only touched the ball once on the drive for a 12-yard run. Still, they got close enough for Eddie Murray to try for a field goal from only 23 yards out. He missed!

When the Lions got the ball back, Barry took a handoff from Erik Kramer. He was stopped by defensive end Chris Doleman after a one-yard gain. The Lion coaches knew that Barry was the man they needed to get the ball to. They called for two short passes in a row — one for eight yards and one for four yards — to get Barry the ball in the open field. As Barry says "That's what I do best — get into the open field and make things happen."

He did make things happen. On second down from the Viking 45-yard line, Barry took a handoff from Erik Kramer. He broke through the Minnesota line and was off. Barry outran the Minnesota defenders to the end zone for a 45-yard touchdown! The score was 17–7 on Barry's second touchdown, and he wasn't finished yet.

The Lions quickly got the ball back on an interception, and they went right back to Barry. He took the first handoff for nine yards. He ran for 11 more yards on his next carry. Barry was in the zone. Minnesota couldn't find a way to stop him. "He's the best pure runner in the league," said Viking defender Henry Thomas after the game. "No matter what we tried to do, he crossed us up."

After a short rest, Barry caught a pass for 13 yards to get the ball inside the Viking 10-yard line. On the play, linebacker Jimmy Williams was called for roughing the passer and the Lions were given the ball on the four-yard line. Barry then took the handoff and snuck behind the left side of the lines into the end zone. Touchdown! It was Barry's third for the day, and the Lions were leading, 24–7.

The Vikings, however, had not given up. Early in the fourth quarter, they scored. That cut the Lion lead to 10 points with more than 11 minutes left in the game.

What did the Lions do? They put the ball right back into the hands of Barry Sanders. He ran the ball four straight times, finally scoring on a nine-yard run. Four plays, 59 yards, and touchdown number four for Barry. It was a career high for him. (The last player to score four touchdowns in a game against the Minnesota Vikings was Hall of Famer Gale Sayers of the Chicago Bears, in 1965.)

The Lions held on and won the game, 34–14. Since the Chicago Bears lost that day, the win put the Lions within one game of the NFC Central Division lead.

Barry finished the game with 23 rushes for 220 yards — the most he had ever gained as a pro up to that point. He broke the Lions' team record of 198 yards. It had been set by Bob Hoernschemeyer 41 years earlier!

Barry's teammates knew that they had seen one of the NFL's greatest players give one of his greatest performances. Lineman Lomas Brown said, "I think we should cherish these moments watching him run, because I don't think you'll see another like him in a long time."

Barry was named NFC Offensive Player of the Week. He also reached the 1,000-yard mark, becoming the eighth running back in NFL history to rush for more than 1,000 yards in each of his first three seasons.

What's also amazing about Barry is that he's doing spectacular things in a big guys' game. Barry Sanders is 5' 8" tall and weighs only 203 pounds. But he has never let his size keep him from reaching his goals.

"Football is played by many shapes, sizes, and colors

and there are a lot of small guys that are very good at it. Sometimes those guys are your best players," Barry explained after the 1994 season. "It doesn't matter how big or tall or wide you are, it has to do with your desire and ability to play the game."

Barry has giant-size portions of desire and ability. He has come a long way since the days when he couldn't even make the starting lineup of his high school football team.

HEAD TO HEAD

Since 1989, no NFL running back has rushed for more yards than Barry Sanders. Barry's total since 1989 is 8,672 yards. Thurman Thomas of the Buffalo Bills is second with 7,843 yards and Emmitt Smith of the Cowboys is third with 7,183 yards. They are all chasing the all-time record of 16,726 yards, set by Walter Payton.

2

THE KING OF KEEP-AWAY

Barry was born in Wichita, Kansas, on July 16, 1968. Wichita is in the southern part of Kansas. It's about a one-hour drive from the Kansas-Oklahoma border. It is a small city of 289,000 people. Wichita is famous for being the cradle of the airline industry and for its animal stockyards.

As a kid, Barry was never lonely. He was always surrounded by members of his big family. His parents, William and Shirley Sanders, had 11 kids. Barry had eight sisters: Ardalia, Helen, Nancy, Gloria, Donna, Gina Marie, Elissa, and Krista. He also has two brothers: Boyd and Byron. Barry was the seventh child born in the family.

Barry's family lived in a small house in Wichita. It was a busy, crowded household. Maybe Barry got his great speed from racing everyone to the dinner table!

When the kids got rowdy, William Sanders would to put his foot down quickly. He loved his family, but he was very strict. He expected his kids to work hard in school and keep out of trouble.

For the most part, Barry listened to his dad. He was an average student in school. He especially liked math. But he and his brother Byron, who is a year older, did get into trouble a few times when they were young.

"I'm not perfect," Barry once told a reporter. "When I was younger, people thought I was a bully. Byron and I stole candy and got into a lot of fights at school." Barry straightened himself out because of his oldest brother, Boyd. Boyd got into a lot of trouble when he was younger. He used to sneak out of the house late at night and not come home until early morning. His dad caught him and had a talk with him to make him change his ways. When Boyd got older, he became a minister.

Boyd set an example for Barry and Byron. "They saw me get into trouble," says Boyd, "and they said to themselves, 'That's not what I want to do.'"

Barry's father loves football. Since Wichita is close to Oklahoma, Mr. Sanders grew up rooting for the University of Oklahoma football team. It was one of the best teams in the country for many years.

Barry and Byron spent many Saturday afternoons watching the University of Oklahoma football team on TV with their father. In 1978, Oklahoma had a running back named Billy Sims. He was Barry's favorite player. Billy won the Heisman Trophy, which is awarded each year to the best college player in the country. Barry watched Billy and wished he could play for the University of Oklahoma and win the Heisman Trophy.

When Barry was young, he was usually small for his age. Sometimes he worried that he wouldn't be able to play football because of his size. "At an earlier age, I wanted to be bigger because [I thought] that you have to be big to play football," Barry remembers. "Then I realized there is a place for the small man."

Before he played organized football, Barry and his friends played "keep-away." In this game, everyone tries to tackle the kid who has the ball. Since Barry was usually the smallest kid in the group, he couldn't just break through tackles, like the bigger kids would.

"Instead of running through all the kids," Barry says, "I had to run around and arch my back and twist and turn and do everything I could to make it." It helped Barry learn the kinds of moves he uses to avoid tacklers today.

Besides keep-away, Barry also loved to play basketball — another tough sport for a little guy! When he was in first grade, his father signed up Barry and Byron in a kids' league. Barry has been playing ever since. It's also his favorite sport to watch.

Barry started playing football with his friends in the neighborhood. Many of them were bigger and older than Barry was. Sometimes there would be as many as 20 players on a team.

"From fourth grade on, I was always smaller than

most kids," he says. "It was intimidating, but I liked the game and I wanted to play."

When he got to junior high school, Barry played in the Greater Wichita Athletic League, the local pee-wee league. His brother Byron played in the same league. Barry was a consistent player. But Byron, who was a little bigger than Barry, usually got most of the attention. Barry didn't let that bother him. He was just happy to be on the team.

Barry did more than play sports. He and his brothers and sisters also liked to play church. The other kids would be the choir, and Barry would pretend to be the preacher. He held a Bible high above his head and spoke like his favorite church preacher, Father Greg Franklin.

The Sanders were a very religious family. Every Sunday, they went to Wichita's Paradise Baptist Church. During the summers, Barry's mom ran what she called Vacation Bible School. She would invite kids from the neighborhood to come to the Sanders house and read the Bible. Mrs. Sanders would give the kids candy if they learned their Bible verses. Barry loved candy, so he always studied hard.

Barry loved to eat. He burned up everything he ate, though, because he was always running around and playing sports. But he chowed down every chance he got. His favorite foods were chicken and chocolate snack cakes.

One summer, when Barry was 10 and Byron was 11,

their father bought a lawnmower for them. Then he helped them find places to mow lawns for money. On their first day out with the mower, the boys mowed a lot of lawns.

"They worked all day," Boyd remembers, "but they came home with no money." They had spent it all on food! "You could never feed those guys enough!" Boyd says. The next day, Mr. Sanders helped the boys make a budget, so they could save some of their money.

Barry's parents taught him a lot about the importance of hard work. His father worked as a carpenter. He earned enough money to support the family, but he wasn't rich. Although the Sanders family lived in a nice neighborhood, Mr. Sanders wanted his children to do better than he had. He wanted them to go to college and get a good education, which would lead to high-paying jobs.

Barry's mother also knew the meaning of hard work. While she was raising her 11 kids, Mrs. Sanders found time to go to college. Mrs. Sanders had started nursing school before she got married and wanted to go back to finish. She returned to school in 1977, when Barry was 9. Finally, in 1982, she achieved her goal. She graduated from college and got a job as a nurse.

Barry was impressed by his parents' hard work. "Seeing my mom and dad raise 11 kids, against the odds they faced, gave me confidence in what I could do," he says.

From an early age, Barry was confident that he could play football. But when he got to high school, the coaches weren't so sure. Barry would have to prove that he was good enough to play high school football. It wouldn't be easy. There was one Sanders boy on the team already. It was Barry's big brother, Byron. He was a running back and one of the team's best players. Was the varsity team big enough for both of them?

HEAD TO HEAD

Barry was born in Wichita, Kansas. Wichita is also the birthplace of Gale Sayers, one of the greatest running backs in history. Gale played for the Chicago Bears from 1965 to 1971. He entered the Pro Football Hall of Fame in 1977. Barry came along too late to see Gale play. Instead, the players he idolized as a kid were Tony Dorsett, O.J. Simpson, Greg Pruitt, Earl Campbell, and Terry Metcalf.

BYRON'S BACKUP

Playing football for North High School was a Sanders family tradition. Barry's father had played for the varsity team when he was in high school. Barry's brother Byron joined the varsity squad as a sophomore. And in the fall of 1983, Barry joined the North High School Redskins sophomore team.

Barry began his first year as the starting running back. Byron was already starting and starring on the varsity team. Did that bother Barry? No way! He was glad that his big brother was doing well.

Byron was bigger and stronger than Barry. He overpowered defenders by running straight up the middle. He was very talented and would make second-team all-Kansas as a junior (but he missed most of his senior season with an ankle injury).

Barry was only about 5' 6" tall and weighed less than 160 pounds. Some of Barry's coaches were afraid that he was too small to be successful as a running back.

But this quiet, little kid was full of surprises. The sophomore coach, Kyle Sanders (who is not related to

Barry), remembers one game in particular. North High was playing its crosstown rival, East High School. Late in the game, East was ahead by four points. Barry took a handoff, ran to his right, then threw the ball to the tight end for a touchdown! North won the game, 18–14.

"It was a perfect pass," says Coach Sanders. "A perfect spiral."

The next year, Barry made the varsity team. Instead of running back, he played wide receiver and defensive back. There were three reasons for this.

First, the coaches thought Barry was too small to play running back on the varsity level.

Second, Barry liked to dance around to avoid tacklers, so the coaches thought he was afraid to run up the middle. They wanted straight-ahead runners like Byron. (Barry *wasn't* afraid. The way he saw it, why run up the middle, where you know you're going to get hit, when you can get to the outside and outrun everybody?)

The third reason was a more personal one. Byron was still on the varsity team. Barry liked the idea of playing alongside his brother, but he did not want to compete against him for a starting job. So he didn't really push to be the starting running back.

From the start, North coaches didn't have much confidence in Barry. "I never knew how good I could be because everyone was always telling me I was too small to be much," Barry said. "Everyone but my father. He told me

I could be great. I know people think that is just a [proud] father talking, but he always told me the truth."

After Byron graduated from high school, Barry hoped to become the Redskins starting running back. A new coach, Dale Burkholder, had taken over the team. To start at running back, he chose the player who had filled in for Byron when Byron was injured his senior year.

It was a setback for Barry, but he didn't let it get to him. Instead, it made him even more determined. "He just worked harder," says Gina Sanders, one of his younger sisters. "He had a lot of hope that he would eventually play."

In the first game of his senior season, Barry played wingback, a receiver position. He did get to run the ball three times — and he scored a touchdown each time! The North High Redskins defeated Topeka West.

Coach Burkholder began to have Barry practice at running back. In the third game of the season, against Wichita Southeast, Barry finally got his chance. During the game, the coach sent Barry in at running back to replace the starter. On his second carry, Barry ran into the open and scored a 45-yard touchdown!

By the fourth game of Barry's senior year, Coach Burkeholder made Barry the starting running back. Barry went on to rush for more than 1,000 yards in the last five games of the season. He finished the year with 1,417 yards.

Barry led the Redskins to the state playoffs that year.

They came close to beating one of the best schools in the state — Manhattan High School, of Manhattan, Kansas. On a very muddy field, Barry ran for 117 yards and leaped over a defender to make a spectacular catch for a touchdown. The final score was Manhattan 16, Wichita North 14.

When the football season was over, Barry went right into basketball. He played on the varsity team for two years. Barry was the starting point guard and the co-captain of the Redskins varsity squad. But his dad wanted him to focus on football, since there were more college scholarships offered for football than for basketball.

It took a while, but Barry had finally proven himself in high school. His athletic feats, combined with his modesty, made him popular with his classmates. They even voted him Homecoming King!

"He always had a smile on his face," says Coach Sanders. "He was just a nice, nice kid."

Although he had become a high school sports hero, Barry continued to work hard to improve. He worked out at the community center down the street from his home all the time. He and Byron would lift weights to build their strength and endurance. "In about seventh or eighth grade I discovered weights," says Barry. "I was devoted."

Barry and Byron would also go to Wichita State University to work out. There they would run up and down the stadium steps to keep in shape.

Now that his high school career was behind him, it was time to think about college. Barry wanted to play college football somewhere. But where?

Since he had been a starter for less than half a season, not many college coaches had seen Barry play. Coach Burkeholder tried to help Barry get recruited. He put together a highlight video of North High's season and sent it to college coaches in the area. Barry was involved in almost every play. Even though the tape was impressive, most college coaches ignored Barry. They thought he was too small. (He was now 5' 8" tall and 175 pounds.)

"We didn't even look at him," says Woody Widenhofer, who was the head coach at the University of Missouri at the time. "I don't think too many schools did."

The schools that were really interested in Barry were Emporia State (a small college in Kansas), Iowa State University, the University of Tulsa (in Oklahoma), and Oklahoma State University (OSU). OSU had actually stumbled upon Barry. An OSU scout had been recruiting one of North High's linemen and had seen Barry play.

Later, George Walstad, an assistant coach at Oklahoma State, saw the tape of Barry. He though the little running back was something special and wanted to recruit him. George kept the tape for two weeks, because he was afraid other schools would see it and want Barry, too!

All of these schools offered Barry a full athletic scholarship to attend their school and play football. Barry's parents let him make the decision on where to go. He chose Oklahoma State University because he liked the team and the coaches a lot.

Barry's parents wanted him to do more in college than play football. His father gave him this serious advice: "Don't dare come back here in four years high-fiving and hollering about what you have done on some football field," Mr. Sanders told his son. "Come back with a job and an education. If you are going to come back and be like me, don't even go."

Barry took that advice seriously. He wasn't thinking about going from OSU into the National Football League. He wasn't even sure he was good enough to compete on the college level. Late that summer, he left for Oklahoma State, ready to work hard — in the classroom and on the football field.

HEAD TO HEAD

While Barry was just becoming a star running back for North High School in his senior year (1985), Emmitt Smith was already the star running back for Escambia High School, near Pensacola, Florida. Emmitt was a year younger than Barry, but he had been the starting running back for Escambia since he was a freshman. By his senior year, Emmitt helped Escambia win two state championships.

4
WAITING
IN THE WINGS

In the fall of 1986, Barry moved to Stillwater, Oklahoma, home of Oklahoma State University (OSU). Barry knew that OSU had some very talented players on its football team, which meant he wouldn't be the center of attention. That was okay with Barry; he just wanted to fit in.

Barry didn't play much at running back during his freshman and sophomore seasons. He was the backup to OSU's star runner, Thurman Thomas. Thurman was one of the best college running backs in the country. He would later become an NFL star with the Buffalo Bills.

Barry carried the ball only 74 times in 1986, playing whenever Thurman needed to rest. The OSU Cowboys finished the 1986 season with a 6–5 record. Barry wasn't worried about his playing time. He kept busy studying for a degree in business.

OSU Coach Pat Jones hoped to get Barry more playing time in 1987. With Thurman returning at running back, the coach made Barry his kickoff and punt return specialist.

It turned out to be a great move. In the first game of the season, against Tulsa, Barry took the opening kickoff and sprinted 100 yards for a touchdown. Oklahoma defeated Tulsa, 39–28. Barry was so good at returning kicks that Coach Jones wanted him to play more at running back. After the seventh game of the season, Coach Jones announced that Thurman and Barry would alternate at running back each time the Cowboys went on offense.

I n early November, the Cowboys were scheduled to play the University of Oklahoma. Oklahoma was one of the nation's best teams in 1987. OSU lost, 29–10, but Barry had a good day. In the fourth quarter, he scored on a one-yard run. It was the first touchdown OSU had scored against Oklahoma in three years.

A week later, against Kansas University, Barry had another big game. He returned a kickoff 100 yards for a touchdown. Barry also rushed for 116 yards. In all, Barry gained a total of 263 yards that day. Oklahoma State won big, 49–17.

Barry ended up leading the nation in kickoff returns in 1987 with an average of 31.6 yards per return. He also finished second in the nation in punt returns. His efforts earned him a place on the 1987 All-America team as a kick return specialist. OSU finished the season 9–2 and defeated West Virginia in the Sun Bowl.

When the 1988 season rolled around, it was time for Barry to take center stage. He wasted no time before proving that he could handle the job of starting running back. In the season opener, against Miami University of Ohio, he returned the kickoff on OSU's first possession 100 yards for a touchdown, then rushed for another 182 yards. Oklahoma State won the game, 52–20.

The next week, in a game against Tulsa, Barry really exploded. He carried the ball 33 times for 304 yards and five touchdowns! Oklahoma won, 56–35.

Barry's 304 yards set a new single-game school rushing record, and he found himself leading the nation in both rushing and scoring.

Barry's style was unique. He ran low to the ground, twisting and turning, using his powerful thigh muscles to spring through holes in the defense. And once he got past the first wave of tacklers, he was gone!

The more Barry ran, the more popular he became as a player. When reporters asked him about his success, Barry often gave credit to his teammates. Off the field, he still spent most of his time doing three things — studying, playing basketball with his friends, and sleeping.

"Barry slept more than anyone I've ever known," says Mike Gundy, who was the OSU quarterback at the time. "The guy loved to sleep." Sometimes, Barry even slept in the locker room during halftime of football games.

By early November, football fans and reporters were mentioning Barry as a candidate to win the Heisman Trophy. It is awarded every year to the best player in college football. Barry was averaging more than 200 rushing yards per game. He was also on a pace to break the national record for most rushing yards in a season. (The national record was 2,342 yards. It was set by running back Marcus Allen of the University of Southern California, in 1981.)

Oklahoma State finished the 1988 season with a 9–2 record. The losses came late in the season, against two of the country's best teams: The University of Oklahoma and Nebraska.

Still, Barry kept running wild. Against Oklahoma, he gained 215 yards and scored twice. In the loss to Nebraska, Barry ran for 189 yards and four touchdowns.

By December, there was little doubt Barry would win the Heisman Trophy. Barry said he wanted to win it for his father. "I think my dad would be extremely happy to have a Heisman sitting around in his living room," he said.

Each year, the Heisman winner's name is announced at a ceremony in New York City. The 1988 ceremony was held on December 8. Barry couldn't be there for the ceremony. The Cowboys were in Tokyo, Japan, to play their last game of the season against Texas Tech.

Barry was the first junior to win the Heisman since 1982, when it went to University of Georgia running back Herschel Walker. Herschel went on to become an NFL star.

After the Heisman ceremony, Barry turned his attention back to playing football. He already had 2,296 yards for the season. He needed just 47 yards to break

Marcus Allen's record!

In Tokyo, Barry rushed for his career best 332 yards and four touchdowns against Texas Tech. He finished the season with 2,628 rushing yards and 39 touchdowns. Both numbers were national records. Barry had had the greatest season a running back ever had in college football history!

On December 30, 1988, OSU played the University of Wyoming in the Holiday Bowl, in San Diego, California. Barry carried the ball 29 times for 222 yards and five touchdowns — all Holiday Bowl records. OSU won, 62–14.

Barry had dominated college football for a whole season. He had won the Heisman Trophy, the biggest honor any college football player can receive. He was at the top of his sport. But soon Barry would face a big decision: Should he stay in college or turn pro?

HEAD TO HEAD

When Barry won the Heisman Trophy in 1988, University of Southern California quarterback Rodney Peete finished second. Barry and Rodney then became teammates on the Detroit Lions from 1989 until 1993. The player who finished third in the voting that year was University of California at Los Angeles quarterback Troy Aikman, who was drafted by the Dallas Cowboys.

TIME TO GO

In January, 1989, a scandal rocked Oklahoma State University. The OSU football program had been investigated by the National Collegiate Athletic Association (NCAA). The NCAA makes the rules for college sports and makes sure that schools follow those rules. After the investigation, the NCAA announced that OSU had broken NCAA rules while trying to recruit new players.

The NCAA punished OSU by saying that the school could still play the 1989 season, but its record would not count toward the Big 8 or the national championship. The Cowboys could not appear on television in the coming season and could not play in a bowl game.

Barry had not broken any rules, but he would be punished as part of the team. Barry's father didn't like that. He wanted Barry to leave school and apply for the NFL draft. Mr. Sanders asked "Why risk those legs of gold for nothing?" If Barry got injured his senior year, it would affect his position in the draft.

But Barry's mom wasn't sure he should leave college. "So many things can happen," Mrs. Sanders said. "It's hard to go back to school when you leave it."

Barry agreed with his mom. But he agreed with his dad, too! Barry decided to leave school and try for the NFL. He hoped that someday he would return to college.

At the time, however, the NFL only accepted players who were no longer eligible to play in college. Barry was still eligible for college, so he would not be allowed to enter the NFL draft.

When they got Barry's request to enter the draft, NFL officials reviewed their rule. They decided that it was not fair to keep players out of the NFL draft based only on their time in college. The rule was changed, and Barry was allowed to enter the draft.

In the time leading up to the draft, people in the NFL were watching Barry, on film and in person. One person who was impressed was Wayne Fontes, the new head coach of the Detroit Lions.

The Lions had had a rough year in 1988. They finished the season with a 4–12 record. They needed some changes. Coach Fontes was installing a new offense that called for one running back, instead of the usual two. The coach wanted Barry to be that running back.

On the day of the draft, on April 23, 1989, Coach Fontes got his wish. The Lions had the third pick overall. When their turn came, they didn't have to think twice — they grabbed Barry!

Barry was following in the footsteps of his hero, Billy

Sims. Both had won the Heisman Trophy — and both were drafted by the Lions! When Billy retired in 1984, he was the Lions' all-time leading rusher. Barry hoped to break his rushing record someday.

In May, Barry flew to Detroit for rookie camp. In rookie camp, players come in to get their playbooks, go through physicals, and meet teammates and coaches. Coach Fontes thought he should offer his star rookie special treatment. He told Barry that he was sending a limousine to pick him up at the airport. "No way!" said Barry. He was grateful, but he didn't want to be treated differently.

As the 1989 NFL season approached, the only thing Barry was missing was a contract. Barry's agents, Lamont Smith and David Ware, and Lions owner William Clay Ford (grandson of auto pioneer Henry Ford), talked all summer and tried to reach an agreement about salary. Barry missed all of the Lions' training camp. If he didn't sign a contract soon, he would miss the beginning of the 1989 season.

While he was waiting at home in Wichita, Barry worked out with weights and ran to stay in shape. He also studied the Lions' playbook so he would be ready to go as soon as his contract was signed.

Finally, three days before the season started, Barry signed a contract. He would earn $6.1 million for the next five years, which included a $2.1 million bonus.

Barry donated 10 percent of his signing bonus,

$210,000, to the Paradise Baptist Church in Wichita. It is the church Barry went to while he was growing up.

The Lions kicked off the 1989 season with a game against the Phoenix Cardinals at home, inside the Pontiac Silverdome in Pontiac, Michigan. (Pontiac is a small city outside Detroit.) It was the first game of Barry's professional career. The Lions were hoping to improve, but they weren't given much chance of making the playoffs.

Since Barry had missed training camp, he didn't get into the game until the second half. At the time, the Cardinals were leading the Lions, 6–3.

On his first carry, Barry busted through the middle for an 18-yard gain! When the game was over, Barry had gained 71 yards on just nine attempts, and he scored the Lions' only touchdown. But the Cardinals won, 16–13.

The next week against the New York Giants, Barry was held to just 57 yards rushing but he exploded for 96 yards receiving. It wasn't enough to help the Lions win, though. The final score was Giants 24, Lions 14.

By game three, Barry had hit his stride. Against the Chicago Bears, he broke the 100-yard mark for the first time in his pro career. He carried the ball for 126 yards and a touchdown. But once again the Lions lost, 47–27.

Barry got hurt in that game. He suffered a hip injury that would bother him for many weeks.

By week eight, Barry's hip had healed. In a 23–20

overtime loss to the Green Bay Packers, he rushed for 184 yards. Barry was having a great rookie season. But his personal achievements were overshadowed by all the losing the Lions were doing as a team. Soon, though, Barry would take matters into his own hands.

B y week nine, the Lions were 1–8. On November 12, they finally seemed to be on their way to another win. Late in the game, Detroit was leading Green Bay, 24–20.

On the sideline, Detroit coaches were planning their offensive strategy. "I don't care what you do," Coach Fontes told his assistants. "Just give the ball to Barry!"

The Lions went on offense and handed the ball to Barry six plays in a row. Barry rushed for 53 yards on the drive. On the sixth play, Barry scored! Detroit won, 31–22.

The win was a turning point for the Lions. They went on to win six of their last seven games that season.

On December 24, the Lions played their last game of the season, in Atlanta. With one minute left, Detroit was ahead, 31-24. The Lions had the ball.

Barry had already rushed for 158 yards against the Falcons that day, giving him 1,470 yards for the season. He needed just 10 more yards to pass Christian Okoye of the Kansas City Chiefs and win the NFL rushing title.

Because the Lions had a safe lead, Barry was on the sideline. Backup running back Tony Paige was in the game instead. When Coach Fontes heard how close Barry was to the rushing title, he went up to Barry and asked if he wanted to go in.

Barry shook his head no. Coach Fontes could not believe it. Most running backs would jump at the chance to win the rushing title. Barry had a simple explanation.

"When everyone is out for statistics — for individual fulfillment — that's when trouble starts," Barry explained. "I don't want to ever fall victim to that."

Barry just played hard — and the statistics and honors came to him. At the end of his rookie season, he was named the Lions offensive MVP. He earned a spot on the 1989 Pro Bowl roster, and was honored as the NFL's Rookie of the Year! Barry's first pro season was just a sign of things to come.

HEAD TO HEAD

The same year that Barry was selected by the Lions in the NFL draft, his brother Byron was drafted by the Chicago Bears. Byron had played in college for Northwestern University, in Evanston, Illinois. He ran for 1,062 yards in his final season at Northwestern. The Bears drafted Byron in the ninth round, but he did not make the team.

6
HIGH-FLYIN' LION

The Detroit Lions began the 1990 season with high hopes. They wanted to make the playoffs, something a Lions team hadn't done since 1983. If anyone could lead them to a playoff game, Barry could.

The Lions started off the season on a sour note. They played the Tampa Bay Buccaneers in Detroit and lost 23–20. In fact, Detroit lost seven of its first 10 games. During that stretch, Barry rushed for more than 100 yards in a game only once.

The problem was that the Lions weren't sure who their starting quarterback should be. First, it was Rodney Peete. Then Bob Gagliano was given a chance. Even Andre Ware, their top pick in 1990, got to play some. For the Lions' offense to work, the quarterbacks had to be effective, otherwise, the defense could focus on stopping Barry.

The Lions went on to win three out of their last six games, and finished the season with a 6–10 record. Barry rushed for more than 600 yards in those six games. But by then, the Lions' playoff hopes had disappeared.

Barry, however, was a bright spot in a disappointing

season. He finished with 1,304 yards rushing. That was good enough to lead the league! Barry beat out his old college teammate, Thurman Thomas of the Buffalo Bills, for the NFL rushing championship by just seven yards.

Barry wasn't interested in personal awards, but he got them anyway. He was named to the All-Pro team, and started in the Pro Bowl for the second year in a row.

That offseason, Barry had an experience he would never forget. He agreed to have his picture taken by *Sports Illustrated For Kids* magazine. SI For Kids wanted Barry to pose with a lion for its October, 1991 cover.

On June 26, 1991 Barry was in a photographer's studio in Hollywood, California. That day he would be working with an actor named Josef. Josef was a 500-pound lion!

Barry was scared when he first saw the big cat. Speaking about posing with the lion, he told the photographers, "I want to do it. But I don't want to do it. But I'm going to do it."

When Nik Kleinberg, picture editor from SI For Kids, petted Josef on the head, the lion rolled over onto his back to get his belly rubbed. But Josef was still a wild animal. Someone in the studio moved too quickly and Josef let out a loud roar that practically shook the room! Luckily Barry wasn't in the studio at the time. He might have run out the door and never come back.

Barry and Josef worked well together. Later, Barry

was asked how he felt about posing with Josef. "It was a really good learning experience," he explained. "It was fun but I don't want to do it again."

Back in the world where the only lions he knew were his own teammates, Barry entered the 1991 season as the best running back in football. The Lions were counting on Barry to keep up his amazing rushing pace. Then the unexpected happened. Barry got hurt.

Barry hurt his ribs during a pre-season game against the Kansas City Chiefs. He hoped to play in the season opener against the Washington Redskins, but he was in too much pain. Without Barry, the Lions had no bite. They lost to the Redskins, 45–0.

Barry rested up and let the injury heal. The following week, Detroit played the Green Bay Packers. Barry was still in a lot of pain, but he didn't want to let his teammates down. In the game, he carried the ball 18 times for only 42 yards and a touchdown. The Lions beat the Packers, 23–14.

Feeling stronger every week, Barry followed the Green Bay game with four 100-yard games. What made the streak most satisfying for Barry was that the Lions won all those games. They were finally playing well as a team.

Chris Spielman, one of the best linebackers in the NFL, led the defense. On offense, Barry was no longer the Lions' only weapon. Quarterbacks Rodney Peete and Erik Kramer, both played well. Wide receivers Brett Perriman and Robert Clark were also having solid seasons.

Detroit finished the regular season with a 12–4 record. It earned them first place in the NFC Central Division for the first time since 1983!

Barry finished the season with 1,548 yards rushing. It was the best single-season total he ever had, but it was not the best in the NFL that season.

Emmitt Smith of the Dallas Cowboys had 1,563 yards for the year. He was the 1991 NFL rushing champ.

Barry got the last word a few weeks later. The date was January 5, 1992. The Lions were facing the Dallas Cowboys in the first game of the playoffs. It was Barry's first playoff game ever.

In the game, Emmitt ran for 80 yards, while Barry rushed for 69 yards and a touchdown. Erik Kramer, the Lion quarterback was the real star that day. He completed 29 of 38 passes for 341 yards and three touchdowns. The Detroit defense held Emmitt and the Cowboys to less than 100 rushing yards total. The Lions won, 38–6. It was Detroit's first playoff victory in 34 years!

The next stop for Detroit was the NFC Championship Game. There they would again face the Redskins — this time with a healthy Barry Sanders.

The Redskins were having a great year. Led by quarterback Mark Rypien and wide receivers Gary Clark, Art Monk, and Ricky Sanders, they had finished the regular season with a 14–2 record. This was a big game. The winners would go to the Super Bowl!

Because the Redskins had the better regular season record, the NFC Championship game was played on their home turf — Robert F. Kennedy Stadium, in Washington, D.C.

The Redskins took an early lead and led 17–10 at halftime. Then they exploded for 24 more points in the second half. The Lions were forced to pass a lot as they tried to catch up. Barry carried the ball only 11 times, gaining 44 yards. The Redskins won, 41–10. (They went on to beat the Buffalo Bills in the Super Bowl, 37–24.)

The Lions had gone much farther than anyone had expected them to — to within one game of the Super Bowl. Detroit had a new confidence as a team. Someday, they hoped, they would make it all the way.

HEAD TO HEAD

The Lions' playoff victory over the Cowboys was their first playoff win since 1957, when Detroit won the NFL championship. The Lions won four division titles and three NFL championships in the 1950s. The stars of those teams were quarterback Bobby Layne and running back Doak Walker, who are both in the Pro Football Hall of Fame.

THE LIONS' KING

When the start of the 1992 season rolled around, the Lions were hungry. They had done well the year before, making it to within one step of the Super Bowl. This year, they wanted to go to the NFL championship game!

However, in the first game of the season, the Lions suffered a disappointing turn of events that set the tone for the entire season. The game was against the Bears, in Chicago. The score was, 10–10, with just under 10 minutes left in the fourth quarter. Barry Sanders took a handoff from quarterback Rodney Peete and was stopped by the Bears defense. Or was he? Somehow Barry kept his balance and didn't go down. He spun away from the pileup and scampered 43 yards for the go-ahead touchdown.

With one minute to play, the Lions led, 24–20. But the game wasn't over yet. Bear quarterback Jim Harbaugh rallied his team. On fourth down, from the Lions' 6 yard line, and with only one second left on the clock, he hit wide receiver Tom Waddle with a pass in the end zone. The Bears won, 27–24.

The loss hurt the Lions. For the first time, Rodney

Peete and Barry Sanders had both played very well in the same game, and they still lost. Barry had 109 yards rushing and Rodney threw for 273 yards and two touchdowns.

The Lions bounced back against the Minnesota Vikings the next week, winning their home opener, 31–17. The Detroit defense and special teams played very well. But over the next four games, the Lions went into a tailspin. They lost all four games. Only six games into the season, they had already lost more than they had in all of 1991.

Detroit seemed to get back on track against the Tampa Bay Buccaneers in game seven. Barry scored two touchdowns. The Lions won, 38–7.

But then they lost another three games in a row, including an embarrassing 37–3 loss to the Dallas Cowboys. The Lions had knocked the Cowboys out of the playoffs the season before, and the Cowboys were hungry for revenge. Barry outran Emmitt Smith, 108 yards to 67 yards, but Emmitt scored three touchdowns.

Barry did enjoy one personal highlight in a loss to the Cincinnati Bengals. On November 22, he rushed for 151 yards, bringing his career rushing total to 5,202 yards. That's 96 yards more than his childhood hero Billy Sims had. Barry became Detroit's new all-time rushing leader!

The Lions won three of their last six games in 1992 to finish the season with a 5–11 record. It wasn't enough to get Detroit to the playoffs.

Barry finished fourth in the NFL in rushing, with 1,352 yards, and played in the Pro Bowl for the fourth year in a row. Emmitt Smith won the rushing title for the second year in a row.

There was one plus to the Lions' losing season in 1992: The NFL schedules teams according to how well they did in the season before. Teams with poor records tend to play other teams with poor records. They don't have to face many of the top teams.

The Lions faced an easier schedule in 1993 and they started off in style. In game one, Barry scored on a 26-yard touchdown run just three minutes into the game. The Lions defeated the Atlanta Falcons, 30–13. Barry had 90 yards rushing and 27 more receiving.

Barry had a big day the next week against the New England Patriots. He ran the ball only 12 times but gained 148 yards in the Lions' 19-16 overtime win. That's an amazing 12.3 yards per carry average.

After losing the next week to the New Orleans Saints, 14–3, Barry and the Lions beat the Phoenix Cardinals, 26–20. Detroit rookie running back Derrick Moore ran for a touchdown in the second quarter. It was the first Lions' rushing touchdown that was *not* scored by Barry Sanders since Barry joined the team.

After dropping a game to the Tampa Bay Buccaneers, the Lions won their next three games. Barry was leading the league in rushing. In the Lions' next game against the Green Bay Packers, Barry reached the 1,000-yard mark for the season. He became only the third player to rush for 1,000 yards in each of his first five seasons in the NFL. The other two are Tony Dorsett and Eric Dickerson.

The Lions traditionally play on Thanksgiving Day. Their opponent that year was the Chicago Bears. The Lions were 7–3 coming in and Barry was having his best year, leading the league in rushing with 1,052 yards.

Then, in the third quarter, with the Lions trailing the Bears, Barry injured his left knee. His regular season was over. He hoped that he would be ready for the playoffs — that is, if the Lions could make the playoffs without him.

The Lions lost that game to the Bears, 10–6, but won three of their last five games. They finished as the best team in the NFC Central division.

With Barry out of action, Emmitt Smith came from way behind to win the rushing title. But Barry's spirits were lifted when he signed a new contract. The Lions had signed him to a four-year contract worth more than 17 million dollars. Now Barry was the highest-paid running back in the NFL.

In the first round of the playoffs, the Lions were matched up against the Green Bay Packers. The Packers and Lions had a long and fierce rivalry. They had played against each other 121 times, but this was going to be their first meeting in the playoffs. The big question on everyone's mind: Would Barry be ready?

By game day, Barry's knee was all healed and he was ready to run. He rushed for 169 yards, setting a Lion playoff record!

But the Detroit defense could not hold off the Packers. With less than a minute left to play, Packer quarterback Brett Favre threw a 40-yard touchdown pass to All-Pro wide receiver Sterling Sharpe. The Packers beat the Lions, 28–24. Once again the Lions were going home from the playoffs empty handed.

HEAD TO HEAD

During the 1993 season, Andre Ware sometimes started at quarterback for the Lions. With him at quarterback and Barry at running back, the Lions' starting backfield was made up of Heisman Trophy winners. Andre won the Heisman in 1990, when he was a student at the University of Houston.

BACK ON TOP

At the start of the 1994 season, Barry had a personal goal — to reclaim the NFL rushing crown. He had been the league's best rusher in 1990, but Emmitt Smith had held the title for the next three years. When the season got underway, Barry was on his way to winning the rushing title. The season would prove to be his best yet.

The Lions started off slowly, splitting their first two games of the year. In game three, they played the Dallas Cowboys, winners of two straight Super Bowls. With a national television audience watching, Barry and Emmitt Smith put on quite a show!

With time running out in the first half, the Lions were trailing, 7–3. Detroit was on the 37 yard line in Dallas territory facing a third-down situation. The Lions needed four yards to get a first down and keep the drive alive. That's when the Lions turned to Barry.

Barry took the handoff and ran straight up the middle. He twisted and zipped toward the left sideline. By the time the Cowboys reacted, Barry had turned downfield and gone nine yards. It was good for a first down.

Two plays later, Lion quarterback Scott Mitchell hit Brett Perriman in the right side of the end zone for a 25-yard touchdown. At halftime, the Lions had a 10–7 lead.

Barry kept up his great play in the second half. The Lion offensive was Barry up the middle for five yards, Barry around the right side for 12 yards, Barry to his left side for seven yards! Overall, Barry rushed for 78 yards in the second half.

Barry's skill at running for first downs kept the Cowboy offense off the field for much of the game. Detroit was leading, 17–10, with just over 4 minutes to play. But Emmitt's six-yard touchdown run tied the score. When the clock ran out, the game was tied, 17–17.

As time was running down in the overtime period, Lion kicker Jason Hanson made a 44-yard field goal. The Lions won, 20–17!

Jason's kick put them over the top, but the Lions couldn't have pulled it off without Barry. He had carried the ball a career-high 40 times, for 194 yards. Until then few players could dominate the Cowboys the way Barry did. He did not score any touchdowns, but he helped the Lions win an important game for a team with playoff hopes.

Barry didn't slow down after his big game against Dallas. He had 131 yards and two touchdowns against the New England Patriots, then 166 yards against the Tampa Bay Buccaneers. When the Lions played the

Buccaneers again six weeks later, Barry exploded for 237 yards, his most ever in an NFL game and a Lions team record. The Lions won, 14–9.

The last game of the season, against the Miami Dolphins, was an important one. Detroit was playing for the division championship. However, the game did not go well for the Lions. They lost, 20–27.

Barry finished the season with 1,883 yards. It was the best total in the NFL for the season (and the fourth best in NFL history). Barry was the league's rushing champion!

The loss to the Dolphins cost the Lions the division championship and put them into the playoffs as a wild card team. Once again, they played the Green Bay Packers in the first round.

In that wild card playoff game, something unexpected happened: Barry was held to minus-one yard rushing! What happened? The Packers went after Barry on every play, and the rest of the Lions offense could not get anything going. The Lions lost, 16–12. They were out of the playoffs.

The playoff disappointment could not take away from Barry's spectacular season. He had rushed for more than 1,000 yards and made the Pro Bowl for the sixth time in his NFL career.

After just six seasons, Barry is already in 12th place on the NFL all-time rushing list, with 8,672 yards. (His colon the NFL all-time rushing list, with 8,672 yards. (His college teammate, Thurman Thomas, is 11th.) The all-time leading ground-gainer in NFL history is Walter Payton, with 16,726 yards.

While Barry is not worried about personal achievements, he does want one thing from his football career: He wants to win the Super Bowl. He'll have that goal on his mind when the Lions kick off the 1995 season.

Despite his success on the football field, Barry still prefers to spend the offseason quietly, with family and friends. "I like to watch movies. I like to go bowling," Barry said. "I like the company of good friends. I'm not living a lifestyle of the rich and famous."

He may not act rich and famous, but Barry is both. Since he is a big star, many people are interested in his life. Newspaper and television reporters are always calling him for interviews. Barry is still a quiet person who shies away from attention. "I have a problem being put on a pedestal just because I run fast," Barry said. "There's a lot more to a person than that."

Barry is a lot like the kid he was in Wichita, Kansas. He still goes to church and spends a lot of time with his family. He's still quiet and a little shy. And he still believes what his father always told him as a kid: He is not better than anyone else. Just luckier.

BARRY SANDERS' CAREER STATS

COLLEGE STATS Oklahoma State University

| Season | RUSHING | | | | RECEIVING | | | SCORING |
	Attempts	Yards	Avg.	TD	Rec.	Yards	TD	Points
1986	74	325	4.4	2	-	-	-	-
1987	111	622	5.6	9	4	58	14.7	1
1988	344	2,628	7.6	37	19	106	5.6	0
Total	529	3,575	6.8	48	23	164	7.1	1

NFL STATS Detroit Lions

| Season | RUSHING | | | | RECEIVING | | | SCORING |
	Attempts	Yards	Avg.	TD	Rec.	Yards	TD	Points
1989	280	1,470	5.3	14	24	282	0	84
1990	255	1,304*	5.1	13	36	480	3	96
1991	342	1,548	4.5	16*	41	307	1	102
1992	312	1,352	4.3	9	29	225	1	60
1993	243	1,115	4.6	3	36	205	0	18
1994	331	1,883*	5.7*	7	44	283	1	48
Totals	1,763	8,672	4.9	62	210	1,782	6	408

PLAYOFFS

Season	Attempts	Yards	Avg.	TD	Rec.	Yards	TD	Points
1991	23	113	4.9	1	9	45	1	12
1993	27	169	6.3	0	2	0	1	0
1994	13	-1	-0.1	0	3	4	2	0
Totals	635	281	4.5	1	14	49	4	12

* led league

Barry Sanders led the league in touchdowns in 1991, with 16 TDs.